# The Case Of The

# DOG CAMP MYSTERY

# Look for more great books in

## The New Adventures of MARY-KATE & ASHLEY

# The Case Of The

# DOG CAMP MYSTERY

by Judy Katschke

■HarperEntertainment
*An Imprint of* HarperCollins*Publishers*

A PARACHUTE PRESS BOOK

**PARACHUTE PRESS**

Parachute Publishing, L.L.C.
156 Fifth Avenue
New York, NY 10010

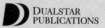
**DUALSTAR PUBLICATIONS**

Dualstar Publications
c/o Thorne and Company
A Professional Law Corporation
1801 Century Park East
Los Angeles, CA 90067

## ⚞HarperEntertainment

*An Imprint of* HarperCollins*Publishers*
10 East 53rd Street, New York, NY 10022

# mary-kateandashley.com

## America Online Keyword: mary-kateandashley

10 9 8 7 6 5 4 3 2 1

# WELCOME TO CAMP BARKAWAY

"**A**rts and crafts, swimming, soccer!" my twin sister, Ashley, said. "Are you sure this camp is for *dogs*?"

"Of course!" Penny Perkins, the camp director, answered. "Clue will have lots of fun at Camp Barkaway. And so will you!"

I looked at Clue, our bassett hound. She was already having fun chewing up my brand-new duffel bag. And *that* was the problem!

Ashley and I run the Olsen and Olsen

Detective Agency from the attic of our house. Clue does a great job of sniffing out clues for us. Lately, though, she's more trouble than help.

"We may be detectives," Ashley said with a sigh. "But we can't figure out why Clue has been acting so strange lately."

"Our only hunch is that we spend so much time on cases," I added. "And we can't always take Clue along."

Penny smiled. "Well, dog camp is just the place for the three of you to be together."

That made me and Ashley feel a lot better. Camp Barkaway wasn't like other dog camps. Besides the fun activities, it had special behavior classes for those dogs who needed them. And right now—Clue needed them bad!

"So tell me what Clue has been doing lately," Penny said. She started walking down the path.

"Well, for starters, she's been chewing

on everything in sight," Ashley said.

"Most dogs enjoy chewing," Penny said.

"Not like this!" Ashley groaned. "Clue chewed our slippers, our books, even our bedroom rug to shreds!"

"She scratches the furniture, tips over her food dishes, and howls at the moon late at night," I added. "She never did that before. It's like living with a floppy-eared werewolf!"

"Maybe you'll want to enroll her in our special doggy manners classes," Penny suggested.

Ashley and I looked at each other. Clue had always had awesome manners. Until now!

Penny took a red bandanna out of her pocket and tied it around Clue's neck.

"What's the bandanna for?" Ashley asked.

"We always give them to our special dogs," Penny explained. She patted Clue's head.

I was about to ask what Penny meant by

"special," when a teenage boy walked over.

Penny smiled. "This is one of our counselors, Tim."

"I've come to fetch your luggage," Tim said. "Fetch...get it?"

Ashley and I groaned.

While Tim carried our bags to our cabin, Penny gave us a tour of the camp. We checked out the fenced-in rings, swimming pond, and activity huts.

Dogs and their owners romped everywhere. It was cool that all the owners were kids—just like us!

"Here is our Paw and Draw hut," Penny said. She led us to a big log cabin. Ashley and I peeked through the door. Dogs were happily slopping paint on paper with their paws. "Maybe Clue will create a masterpiece here."

"Like the...'Bone-a Lisa'!" I joked.

Ashley groaned again.

"And—last but not least—there's the

Camp Barkaway dog show on Saturday," Penny said. "Each year the camp uses ticket sales from the dog show to raise money for animal shelters all over the state."

"But that's only five days away!" I exclaimed. "Who gets to be in the show?"

"All the kids can show off their dogs," Penny explained. "There's a talent show and a big pet parade. And at the end we will give certificates to all of the dogs who pass the manners test on Friday."

"Wow!" I said. "How cool is that?"

But Ashley didn't answer. She seemed to be thinking about something.

"Animal shelters," she said slowly. "Isn't that where dogs and cats go when they don't have homes?"

Penny nodded. She pointed to a pack of happy dogs romping on the grass with their owners. "Most of these dogs were adopted at animal shelters," she said.

Then Penny reached into her pocket and

pulled out two brochures. "Here's a schedule of activities," she said. "In fact, there's a manners class going on right now."

Clue gave a little whine. I could tell she wasn't too thrilled with that idea.

"Have fun," Penny said with a wave. "I'll see you tonight at the Sing-along, Howl-along campfire!"

Ashley and I checked out the schedule. Besides the manners class there was a doggy hike, tug-of-war, and something called Stretch and Fetch.

"What's Stretch and Fetch?" I wondered out loud.

Ashley pointed to a nearby hill. A counselor with a long black ponytail was tossing a Frisbee toward six dogs.

"It must be some kind of doggy workout," Ashley guessed.

"Let's go!" I said, when a German shepherd caught a Frisbee between his teeth. "Clue would love that!"

"Penny suggested the manners class," Ashley reminded me. "And we *do* want Clue to get her certificate at the dog show."

"I know," I said. "But it's Clue's first day at camp. And Stretch and Fetch looks like a blast!"

Ashley smiled. "You're right," she said. "Today is Monday. We'll be here a whole week. That leaves us plenty of time for sit, stay, and heel."

We ran Clue up the hill. A dalmation had just caught a Frisbee and was being hugged by her owner.

Most of the kids smiled when they saw us. But a blond girl about our age with a white standard poodle scowled at Clue.

I walked over to the counselor. "Hi," I said. "My name is Mary-Kate Olsen and this is my sister, Ashley."

Ashley pointed down to Clue. "And this is our dog—"

"Excuse me!" the blond girl called over.

"But that dog is wearing a red bandanna. And I don't want my dog Lacy to be around one of the bad dogs!"

"Now, Grace," the counselor said. "There are no bad dogs at Camp Barkaway. Only those that need a little help."

"Oh, please," Grace said. "Everyone knows that the dogs with the red bandannas don't behave."

"Clue's not *bad*," I put in. "She's *special*."

Clue barked. She raced over to the dalmatian. Then she snatched the Frisbee right out of the dog's mouth.

"Clue!" I scolded. "Give that back!"

No such luck. Clue's long ears bobbed as she darted down the hill with the Frisbee between her teeth.

"You see?" Grace said, jutting out her chin. "I told you she was a bad dog!"

I looked at Ashley. I could tell she was thinking the same thing as I was.

Time for that manners class!

# 2

# THE OFFER

"**N**ow, remember, campers," Rex Vincent, the dog trainer, told us. "It's important to hold your dog's leash firmly. That tells him or her that you are in command."

Ashley and I took turns holding Clue's leash. If Clue was going to ace this manners class, we would have to do everything perfectly.

"And if your doggy does a good job," Rex went on, "reward him with a treat."

Rex pointed to a bag of Bow Wow Chow

dog biscuits behind him. It was propped up against the fence of the manners ring.

"Clue loves chewing on Bow Wow Chow dog biscuits!" Ashley whispered.

"Clue loves chewing on *everything* lately," I whispered back. "That's why we're here!"

I glanced around the ring. All of the dogs were wearing red bandannas. And all of their owners looked very serious.

"Psst," a voice hissed.

Ashley and I turned to our left. A boy with dark brown hair and brown eyes was standing with a chocolate Labrador retriever. The boy's nametag read JESSE.

"What are you in for?" Jesse asked in a low voice.

I nodded at Clue. "Scratching furniture and howling at the moon," I answered.

"How about you?" Ashley asked Jesse.

"Scooter is more stubborn than a mule," Jesse explained. "My parents said I can

only keep him if he gets his manners certificate on Friday."

"Mary-Kate and Ashley!" Rex called out. "It's your turn to walk Clue!"

"I'll go first," I told Ashley.

Gripping the leash, I led Clue to Rex.

"Okay, Mary-Kate," Rex said. "Give the leash a firm tug and say, 'Come, Clue.'"

"Come, Clue," I commanded. I gave her leash a tug, and she began to follow. I gave Ashley a thumbs-up sign.

"Woof!" Clue suddenly jerked the leash so hard I had to let go.

"Clue!" I cried. Our dog ran straight to Scooter. Everyone giggled as the dogs rubbed noses. Everyone except Jesse. He looked pretty mad.

"Hey, it wasn't Scooter's fault!" Jesse insisted. "*That* dog started it." He pointed at Clue.

"It's okay, Jesse," Rex said calmly. "Rubbing noses is a way dogs show affec-

tion. Clue just wants to be friends."

"Scooter didn't come here to make friends." Jesse frowned. "He came here to learn how to behave."

After that, Ashley and I tried hard to keep Clue away from Scooter. But the two dogs definitely wanted to play.

When the class was over, Jesse left without saying good-bye.

"I feel bad," I told Ashley as we headed back to our cabin. "Jesse seemed pretty angry."

"I know," Ashley said. "But if Scooter doesn't earn that manners certificate, Jesse might have to give him away."

That made me feel even worse. I couldn't imagine giving Clue away!

Our cabin was at the end of a gravel path in front of the woods. Inside were two beds, a colorful braided rug, a rocking chair, and a dresser. There was even a puffy doggy bed and a water dish for Clue.

Clue lapped up some water while Ashley and I unpacked our duffel bags.

"Just to be on the safe side," I said as I folded some T-shirts, "we'd better keep Clue away from Scooter at the Sing-along, Howl-along campfire tonight."

"Campfires are the best!" Ashley said, clasping her hands. "Do you think they'll have marshmallows and hot dogs?"

"Of course they'll have hot dogs," I joked. "It's a *dog* camp!"

Suddenly I heard a clatter. Ashley and I spun around and groaned. Clue had tipped her water dish on its side.

"Clue!" Ashley wailed. "Why are you acting like this?"

Clue stuck her nose in the air.

"Come on, Ashley." I sighed. "Let's clean up this mess. Then we can get ready for that campfire."

The Sing-along, Howl-along campfire started at sundown. As the fire crackled, kids roasted marshmallows and ate hot dogs. The canine campers ate special s'mores made with Bow Wow Chow dog biscuits.

Everyone sang along as a guy with a guitar played *Hound Dog, Bingo,* and *Who Let the Dogs Out?* I laughed as I watched a bulldog named Duncan with big wiggly jowls. He was howling up a storm!

"Clue howls, too, you know," Ashley pointed out.

"Yeah," I said. I watched Clue wander over to a group of dogs. "But only when we're trying to sleep!"

I glanced around the campfire at the other kids and their dogs. Grace was there with Lacy. Jesse and Scooter were there, too.

We watched as Scooter flipped open the lid to one of the coolers, took out a soda, and brought it to Jesse.

"That's amazing!" Ashley said. "Clue

doesn't even bring us our slippers."

Suddenly I heard Clue bark. I glanced up and saw her pulling a long string of hot dogs from an open cooler.

"Clue—drop it!" I yelled.

Clue kicked up a cloud of dirt and began running around the campfire.

"Bad news dog!" I heard Jesse mutter as Ashley and I raced past him toward Clue. But it was Penny who finally grabbed her.

"We're sorry, Penny," I said as she brought Clue over.

"That's okay," Penny said. "Clue will learn—"

"I want those squeak toys on my desk in an hour!" a gruff voice interrupted. "No—make that half an hour!"

I turned and saw a grown man walking over. He was wearing a suit and tie. Instead of holding a leash, he was holding a cell phone.

"That's one person who looks out of

place," I whispered to Penny. "Who is that?"

"Oh, that's Hunter Cartright," Penny replied. "He's a very well-known Hollywood commercial producer."

"A Hollywood producer?" Ashley asked. "At Camp Barkaway?"

"Yes," Penny said. "He's staying in the guest cabin while he searches for the next Bow Wow Chow dog!"

"Well, Mr. Cartright's search is over," a voice declared. "*My* dog is the perfect Bow Wow Chow dog."

Ashley and I spun around. Grace was standing behind us with her poodle, Lacy.

"I knew Hunter was going to be here this week," Grace said, smiling. "I read all about it in the *Pampered Poodle Press*!"

"Does Lacy eat Bow Wow Chow?" Penny asked Grace.

Grace sniffed. "Lacy eats only very expensive dog food," she said. "After all, we bought her in a fancy pet store!"

Ashley and I rolled our eyes.

"Lacy has been in five dog shows," Grace went on. "She can walk on her hind legs and play a toy piano." She turned to us. "What does *your* dog do?"

"Clue solves mysteries," I said proudly.

"She's a detective," Ashley added.

"No way! That's imposs—" Grace began. But she was cut off when Hunter suddenly ran over.

"That's the one!" he cried. "My next Bow Wow Chow dog!"

Grace beamed. "I told you," she said to Ashley and me, crossing her arms.

But Hunter walked right past Lacy . . . and straight over to Clue!

"You want *Clue* for your commercial?" Ashley gasped.

"But, Mr. Cartright!" Grace cried. "You don't want *her*."

"Oh?" Hunter asked. "Why not?"

"She's a...bad dog!" Grace said. She

pointed to Clue's red bandanna. "See?"

"She would be perfect in my new commercial," Hunter said. Then he turned away to answer his cell phone.

Grace frowned. "Don't worry," she told her fancy poodle. "No way is that droopy dog going to be in the commercial. Not if *I* can help it." She flounced off with Lacy.

I frowned. What did Grace mean by that?

"So what do you say, girls?" Hunter asked. "Will Clue be our next Bow Wow Chow dog?"

I imagined Clue riding in stretch limos and eating out of crystal doggy dishes. "You bet she will!" I blurted out.

"Where do we sign?" Ashley asked. She looked as excited as I felt.

Penny cleared her throat. "Girls? I'm not sure this is the best time for Clue to be in a commercial."

"Oh...yeah," I said, remembering the

chewed-up furniture and hot-dog raid.

"Thanks, Mr. Cartright," Ashley said. "But Clue isn't . . . uh, feeling well enough to do a commercial right now."

That's for sure. Clue was already digging a huge hole right behind Hunter's back!

Hunter waved his hands at Ashley and me. "Are you kidding? You're passing up fame and fortune here!"

"Thanks," I said politely. "But no, thanks."

Hunter glared at us. Then he spun around and tripped right into the big hole. His face turned red. I couldn't tell whether he was really angry or just embarrassed.

"You're making a big mistake," he said as he climbed out of the hole. "Mark my words—you'll be sorry!"

# BAD DOG!

"**S**top yawning!" Ashley told me the next day. "It's contagious!"

The two of us were standing inside the Manners Ring with a fidgety Clue. Rex was about to begin the class.

"Sorry," I said. "But I'm dog-tired. Clue kept me awake the whole night howling at the moon."

It was Tuesday and our second day at Camp Barkaway. Things didn't seem to be getting any better. Clue was busy barking at something on the other side of the ring.

I looked over and saw Jesse and Scooter. Scooter was straining at his leash to get closer to Clue. Jesse was trying hard to hold him back.

"Good morning, campers!" Rex said. He was wearing plaid shorts, a red T-shirt, and the cleanest white sneakers I had ever seen. "Today we're going to practice the sit command."

I glanced down. Clue was already sitting. A good start!

Just then I heard a rustling noise beside me. I looked over toward the bushes outside the fence.

The top of a blond head and a white poodle tuft were sticking out of the shrubs.

I looked closer. It was Grace! She was holding a pad and pencil. Was she spying on us?

"Mary-Kate and Ashley!" Rex called. "Why don't you try the sit command on Clue?"

"Okay," Ashley said. "My turn." She tugged at Clue's leash and led her over to Rex.

"I'm going to hold up one finger," Rex told Ashley. "And then I'm going to say 'Sit, Clue.'"

Rex cleared his throat. Then he held up his index finger and smiled down at Clue.

"Sit, Clue!" he said. "Sit!"

Clue grunted. She leaned toward Rex's clean white sneaker. And then she began *chewing* it!

I ran to help Ashley pull Clue off Rex's foot.

"Bad dog!" Rex scolded. "I mean— special dog! I mean—"

"We're sorry, Rex," I said. "But Clue has this thing for sneakers lately. New ones."

All the other kids were laughing, except for Jesse. Ashley and I didn't think it was very funny, either. Especially when Rex pulled us aside and spoke to us in a serious voice.

"The Camp Barkaway dog show is in four days," Rex said. "And things don't look good for Clue."

"You mean Clue may not pass the behavior test on Friday?" I gasped.

"Or get her certificate on Saturday?" Ashley asked.

"Not unless she gets some extra care," Rex said. "You might want to take her to see the camp vet."

"But Clue passed the camp physical before she got here," Ashley said. "She had a clean bill of health."

"Clue's problems may not be physical," Rex said in a hushed voice. "They might be inside her head."

"But how can we know what Clue is thinking if she can't talk?" I asked.

"Dr. Russell is an animal expert," Rex said. "Why don't you give him a try?"

"Okay." Ashley sighed. "Anything to help Clue."

"And our sneakers!" I added.

We dragged Clue away from the other dogs and headed straight back to our cabin. "Are you sure we should leave Clue here while we talk to Dr. Russell?" I asked my sister.

"Yes," Ashley said. "Dr. Russell might want to talk to us first. In private."

I gave Clue a pat and shut the cabin door tightly behind me. Ashley and I walked along the main path to Dr. Russell's office.

"Hey, isn't that Jesse?" I asked. I pointed to a boy covered with blue paint who was coming toward us.

"What happened to you?" Ashley asked Jesse.

"I left Scooter in Paw and Draw," Jesse said. "It's usually the only class that calms him down. But today he kicked over a jar of blue paint."

"Accidents happen," I said. I patted Jesse's arm.

"It was no accident," Jesse said. He sounded angry. "Scooter's been acting weird ever since he met Clue."

"But, Jesse—" Ashley started to say.

"My parents are coming to the dog show on Saturday," Jesse interrupted, "to see Scooter get his certificate!"

*Uh-oh*, I thought.

"So keep your wacko dog away from mine before she causes any more trouble," Jesse warned. Then he stalked off.

I tugged Ashley's arm. We had to get to Dr. Russell's office—fast!

"Thanks for meeting with us, Dr. Russell," I told the vet as we sat down. "Clue hasn't been herself lately."

Dr. Russell listened while Ashley and I told him everything—including the chewed sneakers and horrible howling.

"I see," Dr. Russell said, stroking his gray beard. He looked through Clue's records.

"Hmmm. It says here that Clue passed her physical."

"With flying colors!" I added.

"And where is Clue now?" Dr. Russell asked.

"In our cabin," Ashley answered. "We left her playing with her favorite stuffed ladybug."

"Perfect!" Dr. Russell said. "The first thing I would like to do is watch Clue in her natural setting."

We walked back through the camp toward our cabin. Dr. Russell asked some more questions about Clue.

"Was there ever a time in the past when Clue seemed mad at you?" Dr. Russell asked.

"Just once," I said. "When we tried to brush her teeth."

"Until she found out the doggie toothpaste tasted like barbecued chicken," Ashley added. "Then she…"

My sister's voice trailed off. She stopped walking and stared straight ahead.

"Ashley?" I asked. "What's wrong?"

"Mary-Kate, look!" Ashley gasped. "Our cabin door is wide open!"

All three of us ran into the cabin. Ashley and I quickly looked around. Clue's stuffed ladybug was on the floor. But Clue was nowhere in sight!

"Clue?" I called.

"Come out, come out, wherever you are!" Ashley called.

Silence.

"Maybe Clue is hiding," Dr. Russell said. "Some dogs like to get attention that way."

The vet joined Ashley and me as we looked in the bathroom, behind the furniture, and under the beds. We found a few dust bunnies and cobwebs—but no Clue!

"I don't get it," Ashley said. "We made sure to shut the door when we left. And now she's gone!"

"Maybe Clue jumped out of a window!" I suggested.

We ran to check the windows. They were all shut.

"How else could Clue have gotten out?" Ashley asked.

"She couldn't have nudged the door open," I decided. "Not after I shut it so tightly!"

Ashley shook her head. "Then that leaves only one explanation," she said slowly. "Someone *stole* Clue!"

# 4

# CLUELESS

"Clue? Stolen?" I gasped.

"It can't be!" Ashley said. She ran around the cabin again, looking everywhere.

"What are we going to do?" I wailed.

Dr. Russell put an arm around my shoulder. "Don't worry, girls. There's never been a dog stolen from Camp Barkaway."

"Then *where* is Clue?" Ashley cried.

"I'm going to tell Penny," Dr. Russell said. "She'll make sure we find Clue." He hurried out the door.

"It doesn't make sense," I said after Dr. Russell left. "Who would take our dog?"

"*Someone* must have a motive," Ashley said.

A motive is a reason for doing something. Our great-grandma Olive taught us that word. She's a private detective and taught us practically everything we know about detective work. Great-grandma Olive even gave us Clue when she was just a puppy!

"Who would have a motive for stealing Clue?" I asked.

Ashley pulled her detective pad from her duffle bag.

"How about Jesse?" she asked. "He wanted to keep Clue away from Scooter so Scooter would behave."

"Maybe," I said. My eyes darted around the room looking for clues. I spotted Clue's bag of Bow Wow Chow dog biscuits on the dresser.

"What about Hunter?" I asked. "He really wanted Clue for his commercial. And he definitely seemed mad when we said no."

"He also said we'd be sorry," Ashley said. "Could that mean he would steal Clue?"

Ashley added Hunter's name to our list of suspects. Then her eyes lit up. "Speaking of that commercial, I just thought of another suspect," she said.

"Who?" I asked.

"Grace!" Ashley replied. "Remember how she acted when Hunter offered Clue the commercial? She said she'd make sure Clue didn't get it."

"Grace left before we turned down the commercial," I said, nodding. "And it looked like she was spying on us this morning." I filled Ashley in on how I had seen Grace in the bushes.

Ashley added Grace's name to the list. "Three suspects!" she declared. "That's a pretty good start."

"But before we question anybody, let's search the camp," I said. "If Clue *did* leave the cabin on her own, she might be wandering around somewhere."

The door was still open when Ashley and I stepped out of the cabin. But as Ashley turned to shut it, her mouth dropped wide open.

"Oh, no!" she cried. "Look!"

I turned to the door and gasped. Painted in big purple letters were the words: BAD DOG!

# 5

# SNIFFING OUT CLUES

I felt goosebumps on my arms and legs. Who would write such a mean thing on our door?

"The door was open when we came back," Ashley said. "That's probably why we didn't see it."

She moved closer to the door. "Is there anything special about the handwriting?" she asked.

I studied the big purple letters. "The loops on the big *B* are very uneven," I said. "And the small letter *g* ends in a spiral design."

Ashley copied the handwriting onto her pad. I kept staring at the message.

"I know who did it!" I said suddenly. "Jesse had paint all over his hands when we saw him, remember? He must have left the message!"

"Not necessarily," Ashley said. "The paint on Jesse's hands was blue—not purple."

"Oh, yeah," I muttered.

We didn't wash the nasty message off the door. We left it as evidence. We searched all over Camp Barkaway: the pond area, the Stretch and Fetch field, and the Manners Ring. There were lots of dogs everywhere.

But no Clue.

"This whole place is totally Clue-less." I sighed.

Ashley and I were about to rest on a tree stump when we heard music. "Take Me Out to the Ballgame" was blaring over a loud-speaker.

"Where's that coming from?" Ashley asked.

We followed the music to a big outdoor stage. There we saw a Border collie catching a softball between his teeth. The ball was being pitched by a boy wearing a Dodgers cap. About fifteen kids and their dogs were standing in front of the stage watching.

"What's going on?" I asked a girl with a cocker spaniel. The girl was wearing a necklace with the name Helen spelled in colorful beads.

"Rehearsals for the talent show," Helen answered. "I've been here almost an hour waiting for Dribbles to go on."

"An hour?" I asked in surprise.

Helen nodded toward the baseball-playing dog. "Every time he misses the ball, a dozen dogs run to fetch it," she said. "It's out of control!"

I leaned over and petted Dribbles. Then I

felt a dull ache in my chest. Dribbles had long, soft ears. Just like Clue.

"At least all this waiting is for a good cause," Helen went on. "We're going to raise so much money for animal shelters all over the country."

"What will Dribbles do in the show?" Ashley asked.

Helen lifted up a plastic pail of marshmallows. "Dribbles balances marshmallows on his nose," she said.

"Woof!" Dribbles barked proudly.

I tried to smile, but it wasn't easy. Seeing all those dogs made me miss Clue even more.

"Where's your dog?" Helen asked.

"We wish we knew!" Ashley sighed.

"Our dog is missing," I explained. "Her name is Clue and she's a basset hound with a red bandanna. Have you seen her?"

"Nope," Helen replied, petting Dribbles's tail. "Sorry. But I'll let you know if I see her."

"Thanks," Ashley said. We were about to leave when I spotted Grace. She stood on the side of the stage, brushing Lacy with a fancy silver hairbrush.

"Come on," I said to Ashley. "It's time to question our first suspect."

Ashley and I walked up behind Grace. We heard her talking to her poodle.

"Don't worry, Lacy," Grace was saying. "You won't have to worry about that dog Clue anymore."

"Oh, yeah?" I said as we marched over. "Why not?"

Grace jumped. She whirled around to face us. "Because when Hunter sees Lacy looking so pretty, he'll want *her* for that commercial!" she said. "Right, Lacy?"

Lacy let out a low growl.

"Grace," I asked. "Where were you an hour ago?"

Grace twisted the cap off a big gold spray can. "I was right here doing Lacy's

hair. It takes about an hour to get her poodle puff just right. Why do you want to know?"

"Clue is missing," Ashley said.

Grace looked surprised. "Well, I don't know anything about it," she said. She sprayed her dog with a cloud of stinky-smelling hairspray. Lacy sneezed.

"Bless you," I told the dog.

"Now if you'll excuse me," Grace continued. She popped the cap back on the spray can. "Lacy and I have to practice the cha-cha. Come on, Lacy."

Grace gripped Lacy's glittery collar and began leading her away.

That's when I saw it.

Flapping out of the back pocket of Grace's jeans was a bandanna.

A RED bandanna!

# 6

# NUMBER-ONE SUSPECT

"**A**shley, look!" I cried. "That's Clue's bandanna in Grace's pocket!"

I began to run toward Grace. But Ashley grabbed my belt loop and held me back.

"Cool your jets, Mary-Kate," Ashley said. "We don't know for sure if that bandanna is Clue's." She narrowed her eyes. "Although it *does* look suspicious."

"Helen said she was here an hour ago," I remembered aloud. "Let's ask her if Grace was here, too."

Ashley and I walked back to Helen. Her pail of marshmallows was on the ground and her arms were crossed.

"Helen, can we ask you something?" I asked.

Ashley pointed to Grace and Lacy in the distance. "Was that girl and her poodle here an hour ago?" she asked.

"No way," Helen said. "Those two showed up right before you did. Then they started spraying hairspray everywhere. Yuck!"

"Helen Rudaman and Dribbles!" a counselor called out. "You two are next!"

"Yes!" Helen cheered. But when she turned to her dog she gasped. Dribbles and two other dogs were standing over the pail of marshmallows and gobbling them up!

"There goes our act!" Helen wailed.

I felt sorry for Helen. But I couldn't blame Dribbles. Why balance marshmallows on your nose when you could eat them instead?

Ashley and I thanked Helen. Then we

walked off to talk things over.

"The message on our door says 'bad dog'," Ashley said. "That's what Grace has been calling Clue ever since she saw the bandanna around Clue's neck."

"And suddenly a red bandanna shows up in Grace's pocket," I added. "Hmm. Coincidence? I don't think so."

"And if Grace wasn't at the rehearsal an hour ago, she could have been at our cabin," Ashley said.

"So Grace is our number-one suspect!" I declared.

We started back down the path to our cabin. Suddenly a big brown Labrador jumped in front of us.

"Scooter!" I exclaimed.

Scooter panted wildly. He was about to jump on Ashley when Jesse tugged on his leash and dragged him back.

"Jesse?" I said. "Can we ask you something?"

"Sure," Jesse scoffed. "As long as you're not with that bad-news dog."

Ashley planted her hands on her hips. "Jesse, where were you a little over an hour ago?" she demanded.

"You saw me," Jesse said, shrugging. "I was going to my cabin to wash all that gloppy blue paint from my hands."

"Woof!" Scooter barked. He gave his leash a strong tug. Then he jumped up on me, practically knocking me over.

"Oh, no!" Jesse cried. "Down, Scooter!"

Scooter looked into my face and whined.

"What's the matter, boy?" I asked gently.

"He's been like this all day," Jesse said. "Worse than usual. He actually tried to drag me into the woods."

"And Clue isn't even around!" Ashley pointed out.

"You see?" I told Jesse. "Clue wasn't making Scooter do bad things after all."

Jesse looked around. "Where is that

crazy dog of yours anyway?" he asked.

"Clue has been kidnapped." I raised an eyebrow as I studied Jesse. "Do you know anything about it?"

"Gee, no," Jesse said. He gripped the Labrador's collar and tugged him away. "Hope you find her, though."

"Poor Scooter," I said to Ashley. "He looked pretty upset."

"You'll be upset, too, when you see your pants!" Ashley said.

Huh? I looked down and groaned. Scooter had left big blue paw smudges all over my shorts. The stains were flaky and not too wet, but they still left a mess!

"Yuck!" I said. "I guess Scooter forgot to wash up after Paw and Draw."

"You can take care of it when we get back to the cabin," Ashley suggested.

We fell into step. "So Jesse said he was washing his hands when Clue disappeared," Ashley said. "What do you think?"

"For a whole hour?" I replied. "Even Mom doesn't make us wash our hands that long. No matter how messy we get."

"I know," Ashley agreed. "Jesse's story doesn't seem right to me, either."

When we reached our cabin, the "bad dog" message was still on the door. But I noticed something else—a tiny smudge of blue paint on the door handle!

"Look!" I told Ashley, pointing to the handle. "*Blue* paint this time!"

Ashley carefully touched the blue smudge.

"It's dry," she said. "Which means it's been here for a while. But why didn't we see it before?"

"We were probably too busy staring at the creepy message to notice it," I said.

"It leads us straight to one of our suspects!" Ashley said.

Ashley and I looked at each other. *Jesse!*

# 7

# THE PERFECT DOG

"**A**shley!" I cried. "Jesse is our number one suspect!"

"I thought Grace was our number one suspect," Ashley pointed out.

"Oh…yeah," I said. I paused. "Can we have *two* number one suspects?"

"That's a question for Great-grandma Olive." Ashley sighed. "I sure hope Clue is okay. Where could she be?"

I could hear some of the counselors calling Clue's name. It made me feel better that they were all searching, too.

"Well, I don't know, but we're going to find her," I said. I snapped my fingers. "Why don't we get handwriting samples from our suspects? Then we can compare them to the message."

I could practically see the wheels spinning in Ashley's head. "I know how to get samples," she said. "All campers have to write their names on a sign-up sheet before every activity!"

"Except Hunter," I pointed out.

Ashley narrowed her eyes. "In that case," she said, "we'll just have to ask the famous Hunter Cartright for his autograph."

"Ashley!" I complained. "Hunter Cartright makes dog-food commercials. He's not some kind of superstar!"

"But he *thinks* he is," Ashley said, grinning. "He'll do it for sure!"

"I like it," I said slowly. "I like it!"

Ashley quickly tore a clean piece of

paper from her notepad. Then the two of us searched the camp for Mr. Cartright.

"There he is!" Ashley said, pointing. "By the pond!"

I turned to see where Ashley was pointing. All I saw was the back of a lawn chair and a pair of feet in shiny black shoes.

"How do you know it's him?" I asked.

"Who else wears shiny black shoes at camp?" Ashley asked.

"Maybe we should practice before we go over there," I said. I clasped my hands and spoke in a squeaky, pretend-excited voice.

"Oh, Mr. Cartright!" I gushed. "I've seen *all* of your commercials. We'd just *love* to have your autograph!"

Ashley giggled. "Perfect!"

As we tiptoed up behind the chair, I heard Hunter talking on a cell phone.

"I've told you a million times, Diane!" he said. "It's all taken care of. I'll be back in the studio with the perfect dog for the commercial first thing tomorrow morning!"

Perfect dog? Tomorrow morning?

I felt Ashley squeeze my hand. *Was Hunter talking about Clue?*

"And remember," we heard Hunter say. "We'll reveal the new Bow Wow Chow dog to the world with our commercial. Until then, it's top secret."

Hunter stood up and slipped his phone into his pocket. Then he began walking briskly toward the guest cabin.

"Top secret!" I whispered angrily. "Could that be because he *stole* a dog?"

"And you heard what he said," Ashley whispered back. "He's leaving with the dog tomorrow morning. If Hunter has Clue, then we have to get her back, fast!"

"I say we search Hunter's cabin," I said. "Tonight!"

# 8

# TOO MANY SUSPECTS!

**"T***hree* number one suspects!" I said to Ashley during dinner. "Wait until Great-grandma Olive hears about this!"

Ashley nodded as she chewed on a carrot stick. I knew she was thinking about our next plan of action—searching Hunter's cabin for Clue!

I looked around the mess hall. Campers sat at long tables covered with plastic tablecloths. The walls were decorated with Paw and Draw paintings and photos of past dog shows. Windows overlooked a big pen where hungry canine campers ate their dinners.

Clue must be hungry, too, I thought sadly. Wherever she is.

"Attention everyone!" Penny called from a podium. "I have an announcement to make. One of our fellow campers is missing. Our basset hound friend, Clue."

Concerned whispers filled the mess hall. I could hear Scooter howling outside.

"Poor Scooter," I whispered to Ashley. "I think he's really upset that Clue is missing."

"At least *somebody* is," Ashley whispered back. She nodded toward the next table. Jesse was buttering a roll and scowling. Grace looked bored as she stabbed her macaroni with a fork. Hunter was hungrily eating a Caesar salad.

"The counselors, Dr. Russell, and I are all taking turns looking for Clue," Penny told the campers. "But I want all of you to

keep an eye out for her, too."

"Mary-Kate," Ashley whispered. "Hunter is almost finished with his salad. If we want to search his cabin, we have to do it right now."

"Gotcha," I said. Then I raised my hand.

"Yes, Mary-Kate?" Penny asked from the podium.

"Ashley and I want to go back to our cabin to get a picture of Clue," I said. "It might help with the search."

"Okay, girls," Penny said, nodding. "Good idea."

I looked over at Hunter. He was already on his cherry pie. We had to get out of there—fast!

In a flash Ashley and I were out the door. Our feet crunched on the gravel as we hurried down the main path.

"Don't worry, Clue," I said softly when we reached Hunter's cabin. "We're on our way!"

I pulled on the doorknob. Nothing happened. "Rats," I said. "Hunter must have

locked it before he went to dinner."

"Of course he did," Ashley said. "If he has Clue inside the cabin, he wouldn't want anyone to find her."

I ran to a window and tried to peek inside. Even when I stood on my toes it was too high.

"Give me a boost!" I told Ashley.

"You mean step on my hands with your muddy shoes?" Ashley cried. "No way!"

"Okay, okay," I said. "Then I'll give *you* a boost!"

I webbed my fingers together and leaned over. Ashley carefully stepped up on my hands.

"One…two…" I grunted. "Three!"

I pushed Ashley up to the window. She grabbed the windowsill as she peered into the cabin.

"Oh, no!" Ashley gasped.

"What? What?" I asked. I jumped up and down, trying to catch a glimpse.

Ashley glanced down at me.

"It's a dog crate!" Ashley answered. "And I'll bet Clue's inside!"

Ashley opened the window. "Push me in, Mary-Kate!"

I gave Ashley the biggest boost ever. "Oof!" I grunted. My sister popped through the window and landed inside with a *THUD*.

"Ashley?" I called. "Are you okay?"

"I'm fine," Ashley hissed back. "I landed on a bag of Bow Wow Chow."

"Quick!" I called. "Let me in!"

In a flash the front door flew open, and Ashley waved me inside.

The crate sat in the middle of the cabin. We ran over to it. I bent down to look inside.

"Don't worry, Clue," I said excitedly. "We're going to get you out of—"

"Looking for something, girls?" a gruff voice asked.

Ashley and I spun around. *Hunter!*

## THAT'S SHOW BIZ

**H**unter glared at us from the doorway. He looked really, really mad.

Ashley gulped. "We were looking for our dog, Clue," she said bravely.

"And we found her!" I exclaimed. I opened the door to the crate. But the dog that walked out wasn't Clue. It was—

"*Duncan*!" Ashley and I cried at the same time.

The big bulldog slobbered as he looked up at Ashley and me.

"We…we heard you say that you were delivering the perfect dog to Hollywood tomorrow," I said.

"I am!" Hunter said. He pointed to Duncan. "Meet the next Bow Wow Chow dog!"

"Him?" Ashley squeaked.

"Picture it," Hunter said. "Our slogan of the future: Your dog will drool for Bow Wow Chow."

"But he's so different from Clue," I pointed out.

"Things change pretty fast in showbiz," Hunter said with a shrug. "Besides, I was lucky to find a well-behaved dog with an owner that could keep this a secret. This camp is full of ankle biters."

Hunter hiked up the leg of his pants. Right above his ankle was a pair of teeth marks!

"Who did that?" I gasped.

"That nasty poodle Lacy!" Hunter said.

**59**

"She kept trying to take a chomp out of me, and she finally did it!"

"Lacy?" I said. "But she's supposed to be perfectly behaved."

"My ankle doesn't seem to think so," Hunter replied. "Now, if you'll excuse me," he said, reaching into his pocket. "This dog deserves a Bow Wow Chow dog biscuit!"

Hunter waved a biscuit over Duncan's crate. But the bulldog didn't beg. He lay down and covered his eyes with his paws.

"Aw, come on, Duncan baby!" Hunter wailed. "Work with me! Work with me!"

Ashley and I left the cabin, totally confused.

"I guess Hunter *didn't* steal Clue," Ashley said.

We sat on a bench by the pond. Ashley took out her pad and crossed Hunter's name off our suspect list.

"That leaves us with Jesse and Grace," I said.

"Okay," Ashley said. "So if one of *them* took Clue, where would they hide her?"

"You mean *if* they're hiding her," I pointed out. "Jesse would probably have sent Clue as far away as possible from Scooter."

"And if Grace is hiding Clue, it wouldn't be in her cabin," Ashley said. "Penny told us that the counselors had checked all the cabins before dinner."

Ashley shut her detective pad. We stared quietly at the moon. It wasn't quite full, but it was very bright.

"Penny is probably expecting that picture of Clue," I said. "What should we tell her?"

"That Clue chewed up the pictures, too," Ashley said with a shrug. "Before she disappeared."

Ashley and I couldn't take our eyes off the moon.

"I never thought I'd say this." Ashley sighed. "But I'd give anything to hear

Clue howl at the moon tonight."

"And I'd give anything to see Clue chew up my new sneakers!" I said sadly.

Before we went to sleep, I left one of my sneakers out on the cabin doorstep. It was for Clue in case she found her way back to us.

Ashley and I hardly slept a wink. We kept listening for any sign of Clue. A scratch on the door, a bark—even a sniff. All we heard were owls and a few crickets. And in the morning my sneaker was still there, soggy from the morning dew.

"Let's take Clue's stuffed ladybug with us today," I told Ashley as we got ready to leave our cabin after breakfast. "If we find Clue, she might want it."

"You mean *when* we find Clue!" Ashley said.

Ashley and I got right to work. First we headed for the Paw and Draw hut to check

the sign-up sheet for Jesse's handwriting.

On the way we passed the Manners Ring. Dogs were following their owners in a neat circle. As usual, the bag of Bow Wow Chow dog biscuits was leaning against the fence.

But one thing seemed strange. Grace was lurking in the bushes again, watching the manners class!

"Ashley, look!" I whispered.

We watched as Grace scribbled something on her pad. "Lacy's not with her this time," Ashley said.

I saw Grace slip the pad in her pocket. Then she kneeled down and stretched her arm between two bushes and through the fence.

"Check it out, Ashley," I said, pointing. "Grace is reaching into the bag of Bow Wow Chow dog biscuits!"

Grace grabbed a fistful of biscuits. Then she jumped up and ran away.

"Maybe she's bringing the dog biscuits to Lacy," Ashley suggested.

"No way," I answered. "Grace said her dog doesn't eat Bow Wow Chow, remember? Only the fancy stuff."

Ashley's eyes opened wide.

"Lacy may not like Bow Wow Chow," she said. "But Clue does! Maybe Grace is bringing the biscuits to her!"

Ashley and I followed Grace.

"She's heading for her cabin," Ashley said.

"No, she isn't!" I said as Grace made a sharp turn. "She's headed straight for the woods!"

# A CANINE CONFESSION

**A**shley and I ran into the woods after Grace. The farther we ran, the darker the woods became. Soon we couldn't see Grace anymore. But we could hear her footsteps crunching on the twigs and dried leaves.

Finally the footsteps stopped. "That's a good dog!" I heard Grace say.

Ashley and I followed her voice to a clearing in the woods. We hid behind a thick tree trunk and peeked out.

The dog wasn't Clue! It was Lacy, who was

tied loosely to a skinny tree.

"Now let's get to work, Lacy," Grace said.

"Work?" I whispered to Ashley.

Grace placed the pile of dog biscuits on the ground. She yanked out her pad and studied it. Then she held up one finger. "Lacy, sit!" she commanded. "Sit, girl!"

Now I was really confused. Why was Grace teaching Lacy manners? And why was she doing it in the woods?

Lacy just stood there, looking at Grace.

"Come on, Lacy!" Grace whined. "You did it yesterday!"

The poodle yawned.

"Oh, well." Grace sighed. She tossed Lacy a dog biscuit. "Here's one for trying."

"So much for fancy dog food," Ashley whispered to me. She pointed at Grace's notebook. It was lying against a nearby tree. "You distract Grace. I'm going to look at the handwriting in that notebook."

I nodded. "Okay. Good idea."

Ashley and I stepped out of the trees. Grace seemed pretty surprised to see us.

"What are *you* doing here?" she asked.

"Looking for our dog," I said. I crossed my arms as Ashley slid over to the notebook. "So how do you explain the red bandanna we saw in your back pocket yesterday?"

"R-r-red bandanna?" she stammered. "I don't know what you're talking about."

"Can you explain why this handwriting is the same as the painted message on our cabin door?" Ashley asked. She was flipping through Grace's notebook.

I looked over Ashley's shoulder. Grace's handwriting was full of uneven *B*'s and spirally *G*'s. Just like in the painted message!

"Grace? Did you leave us that message?" I asked. The one that said—BAD DOG?"

Grace's shoulders drooped. She didn't answer right away. But something told me she was about to tell us the truth.

"Okay, so I *did* write the message," she said finally. "And I'm sorry. I know it wasn't very nice. I guess I was mad at Clue for getting picked for that Bow Wow Chow commercial."

"Then where is Clue?" I demanded.

"I have no idea!" Grace cried. "I may have written that message—but I did *not* take your dog!"

"Then what were you doing with a red bandanna in your pocket?" Ashley asked. "Only special dogs wear those."

Grace looked really upset now. Her chin began to quiver, and her eyes filled up with tears. "Lacy *is* a special dog," she said sadly. "Penny gave her the bandanna when we got to Camp Barkaway!"

I stared at Lacy. No wonder she bit Hunter. But I still didn't get it.

"So why didn't you just take Lacy to the manners class?" I asked Grace. "Instead of sneaking around?"

"How could I?" Grace cried. "Then everyone would know she was..."

I gently put a hand on Grace's arm. "Just say it," I said calmly.

"A *bad dog*!" Grace cried. "There. I said it!"

"So how come Lacy didn't have to wear the bandanna?" I asked.

"I lied and told Penny the bandanna itched Lacy and made her scratch," Grace said. "She said Lacy didn't have to wear it, and was I glad!"

"Grace," Ashley said gently. "A lot of dogs need special training. That doesn't mean they're bad."

"I guess," Grace said. "But I couldn't bear for anyone to know the truth about Lacy. Especially Hunter Cartright!"

"So you've been training Lacy yourself," I said.

Grace nodded slowly. "Lacy doesn't even eat fancy dog food," she said. "And we didn't

buy her in a fancy pet store, either. My parents adopted her in a shelter."

"But that's cool, Grace," I said. "Some of the neatest dogs come from shelters."

"What makes a dog special is the way she licks your face and stays with you when you're sad or scared," Ashley said. "Not how fancy she is or what kind of food she likes!"

Grace looked down at Lacy. Then she smiled.

"You're right!" Grace said. "Lacy is a great dog. Even if she can't dance the cha-cha."

I watched as Grace gave Lacy a big hug. I wanted to hug Clue so badly that my arms hurt!

"Come on, Lacy," Grace said. "If we hurry we'll make the next manners class. You might even pass the test on Friday and get that certificate!"

Grace gave us a little wave. Then she and Lacy hurried out of the woods.

"I guess I'm happy for Grace," Ashley said as we watched them leave.

"And sad for us." I sighed. "We still haven't found Clue!"

"We're getting closer, Mary-Kate," Ashley said. "There's only one suspect left: Jesse."

"But if he's the one who did it, how can we find out where he's hiding Clue?" I asked.

Ashley leaned against a tree and sighed. "Too bad Scooter can't talk," she said. "I bet he could tell us where Clue is."

"Maybe Scooter *does* know where Jesse took Clue," I said slowly. "And if we're lucky, maybe he'll lead us to her, too."

Ashley thought for a minute. Then she grinned and gave me a high five.

"You're right, Mary-Kate," Ashley said. "Let's go pay Scooter and Jesse a little visit!"

# 11

# PUPPY LOVE

**A**shley and I ran out of the woods and straight to Jesse's cabin. But before we knocked we pressed our ears against the door and listened.

"Heel, Scooter," I heard Jesse say. "Come on, boy. The big test is on Friday. You know the drill!"

Scooter barked. I heard a shuffling sound on the wooden floor. Then a scratching noise on the door.

"Scooter must know we're here!" Ashley

whispered to me. We quickly stepped back from the door.

Jesse opened the door, and Scooter bounded out. He whined and ran circles around Ashley and me.

"What do you two want now?" Jesse asked. "Did you find your dog? 'Cause if you did, just keep her away from here."

"We want to know where you took Clue, Jesse," I said.

"I didn't take Clue," Jesse insisted. "Why would I want another nuts-o dog anyway?"

I kneeled down in front of Scooter and scratched his ears. "Remember Clue, Scooter?" I asked in a gentle voice.

Ashley pulled out Clue's favorite stuffed toy. She held it under Scooter's nose to sniff.

Scooter's ears perked up. Then he began to bark.

"Take us to her, boy!" I said. "Take us to Clue!"

"Woof!" Scooter barked. He jerked his leash out of Jesse's hand. Then he ran from the cabin at top speed.

"Scooter, stop!" Jesse called.

The three of us chased the Labrador. He darted around the cabin—and straight toward the woods.

"The woods?" I asked, confused.

"But we were just there!" Ashley cried.

We followed Scooter deeper and deeper into the trees. Much deeper than we were before. It was kind of scary.

I could practically hear my heart beating. Where was Scooter going? Was he leading us to Clue?

Suddenly I heard a low, long whine.

Ashley and I froze. We'd know that whine anywhere.

"It's Clue!" Ashley gasped.

We followed the noise through two thick trees with twisted branches. Then I looked down at the leafy ground and gasped.

Lying near a clump of branches was Clue—with her back paw stuck in a blackberry bush!

"Clue!" Ashley and I cried at the same time.

Clue let out a weak howl. Her tail wagged tiredly against the ground. "Poor Clue," I said. Ashley and I ran over to give her a hug.

"Look," Ashley said. She pointed to the blackberries growing from the bush. Underneath the bush was a puddle of water. "At least Clue had something to eat and drink."

"We'd better get her out of here," I said. "Fast!"

Jesse came up. The three of us worked together to get Clue's paw untangled. Scooter tried to knock away the branches with his paw. In just a few seconds our dog was free.

Ashley and I hugged Clue so tightly she

grunted. But when we let her go, she padded over to Scooter.

"Wow!" I said as the two dogs began nuzzling noses. "Scooter and Clue are in love!"

"In love?" Jesse cried, wrinkling his nose.

"They must have run into the woods together on their own," Ashley said. "Clue was never dognapped!"

"I'll bet they ran off when I was washing all that paint from my hands," Jesse decided.

"And when Clue got hurt," I added, "Scooter ran out of the woods and tried to get help."

"And I wouldn't listen." Jesse sighed.

Ashley and I gently tugged Clue away from Scooter. Then I scooped Clue in my arms and we hurried back to camp.

The moment we reached camp, we took Clue straight to Dr. Russell's office. The vet gave her a thorough exam and brought her back outside.

"Will she be okay, Dr. Russell?" I asked.

Penny was standing with Ashley and me. So were Jesse and Scooter. Even Grace and Lacy had come by to see how Clue was doing.

"Aside from a sore paw, Clue will be just fine," Dr. Russell said.

"Yay!" Jesse and Grace cheered. Scooter nuzzled his nose into Clue's neck. Lacy yawned.

"I am so happy that you found Clue!" Penny gushed. "And just in time for the Camp Barkaway dog show tomorrow."

Ashley and I were really happy, too. But we were still puzzled about something.

"I don't get it," I said. "Scooter may have found Clue. But who opened the door to let her out of the cabin?"

## 12

# AT YOUR SERVICE!

**S**cooter gave a little bark. Then he jumped up on me and wagged his tail.

"Hi, boy," I said. "I just hope you don't have blue paint on your paws this time."

Ashley raised an eyebrow. "Paws…blue paint…" she said, frowning.

"What's up?" Jesse asked. He looked confused.

"Wait a minute," Ashley said slowly. "All this time we were thinking that a *person* opened the door. But maybe it wasn't a person at all." She looked straight at Scooter. "Maybe it was a dog!"

"A dog opening doors?" I joked. "What next? Turning on the TV? Making waffles?"

"Maybe!" Ashley said. She turned to Jesse. "Did you ever teach Scooter how to open a cooler and bring you a soda? Like he did at the campfire the other night?"

"No," Jesse said. "Scooter always brings me things. He even brings me my toothbrush, which can be pretty gross."

"Jesse!" Ashley said, her eyes lighting up. "Was Scooter ever trained to be a service dog?"

"What's that?" Jesse asked.

"Service dogs are trained to help physically challenged people," Ashley explained. "I saw a show about them on TV once. Service dogs lead their owners safely through their homes and neighborhoods."

"They also learn to do everyday tasks,"

Penny added, nodding. "Like turning the lights on and off—"

"And opening doors!" Ashley piped in.

Jesse frowned. "Actually, I think Scooter *did* get some service training. Before my mom and dad adopted him."

"Bingo!" Ashley cried.

"But he never graduated from the program." Jesse sighed. "Probably because he's so stubborn."

"Maybe not, Jesse," Dr. Russell said, shaking his head. "Scooter is probably just waiting for the commands he learned in school."

"In that case," Penny put in, "all we have to do is find out the commands Scooter learned and use them. And then he'll be perfectly well-behaved!"

"Wow!" Jesse exclaimed. "Do you think we can teach Scooter how to clean my room?"

Dr. Russell smiled and shook his head. "I

think that's pushing it," he said.

"Well, thanks, guys," Jesse said, hugging Scooter around the neck. "When my mom and dad hear about this, I bet they'll let me keep Scooter for sure!"

"Especially when he gets his certificate at the dog show," Penny added with a wink. "I have a funny feeling Scooter will pass the behavior test on Friday!"

"Ye-es!" Jesse cheered under his breath.

Dr. Russell smiled down at Clue.

"And as for Clue," he said. "She wasn't acting up on purpose. She just needed a little less work and more play."

Ashley and I stared at Dr. Russell, then at each other.

"Come to think of it," Ashley said softly, "we have been treating Clue more like a partner lately than a pet."

"Even though we love her as one," I added.

"Most dogs love to work," Dr. Russell

said. "But they also love to have fun once in a while."

"So do detectives!" I declared with a grin. "Come on, Ashley. Now that we've solved this case—let's go for a swim. You, me, and *Clue*!"

Clue and her new friends spent the next few days having fun and training for the manners test. All that cramming paid off. On Friday, Clue, Lacy, and Scooter all aced the test!

When Saturday rolled around, all three dogs were ready for the Camp Barkaway dog show—and their certificates!

Lacy was on her best behavior. Not only did she get her manners certificate—she won first prize in the tail-wagging contest.

Scooter was a winner, too. He won the slipper-retrieving challenge. But the most important moment came when Scooter got his certificate. Jesse beamed as his parents cheered from the bleachers. Ashley and I cheered, too. We knew that Jesse and Scooter were going to be together for a long, long time!

Clue was a big part of the show, too. After getting her certificate, she marched in the doggy costume parade. And she was perfectly well-behaved! I smiled down at Clue, who was wearing her cool Sherlock Holmes–type hat and cape, and we walked her around the stage.

"I guess Clue is back to her old self!" Ashley said.

"Yeah," I chuckled, and looked down at my feet. "Too bad my sneakers aren't!"

Clue barked. She knew her sneaker-chewing, moon-howling, dish-tipping days were over.

And so did we!

"Mary-Kate, look how many people are here," Ashley said as more guests took seats on the bleachers. "And they all came

to raise money for animal shelters!"

I looked down at Clue.

"Ashley, do you think maybe Great-grandma Olive adopted Clue at a shelter when she was a puppy?"

"I wouldn't be surprised," Ashley said. "Penny said you can adopt all kinds of great dogs at shelters. Pure breeds…mixed breeds…"

I kneeled down and gave Clue a huge hug.

"Even dogs that grow up to be detectives!"

## Hi from both of us,

Ashley and I were so excited about our friend Samantha's Halloween party. It was going to be a blast! We offered to help Samantha get everything ready. We had cool snacks, awesome decorations, and all the kids from the neighborhood were invited.

But then things started going horribly wrong. The decorations disappeared, and we started getting messages that said the party was doomed! Who—or *what*—was behind it all?

Want to find out more about this creepy caper? Turn the page for a sneak peek at *The New Adventures of Mary-Kate & Ashley: The Case of the Screaming Scarecrow*.

See you next time!

*Mary-Kate Olsen*    *Ashley Olsen*

A sneak peek at our next mystery...

# The Case Of The
# SCREAMING SCARECROW

"Picture this," Patty O'Leary said. "Black cats *everywhere*. Cats on the invitations, cats on the decorations—even cats on the cake!"

I groaned. Patty O'Leary had elected herself party planner for our friend Samantha's Halloween party. But to tell you the truth, none of us liked her ideas very much.

"Don't you think that's going a little, uh...overboard?" Samantha asked Patty.

Patty looked annoyed. "I'm an *expert* on party planning," she said. "I picked out the perfect centerpiece, didn't I?"

"That ugly scarecrow?" Ashley asked.

I shivered just thinking about it. The scarecrow was smiling—but it was creepy.

"Of course," Patty replied. "It will go perfectly with the black cats."

Samantha rolled her eyes. "Um, Patty—" she began.

But she was cut off by the sound of a high-pitched scream!

"What was that?" Ashley cried.

Samantha jumped up and ran toward the front door. We all followed close behind.

Samantha stopped short when she reached the front yard. "Look!" she said. She pointed her finger across the yard.

Ashley gasped. I couldn't believe my eyes.

Our scarecrow decoration was lying twisted on the ground. And its face wasn't smiling—it was frowning!

I went over and looked closely at the scarecrow. "There's a note pinned to it," I said. I ripped off the note.

"What does it say?" Ashley asked.

I gulped nervously. "Beware! Your party is doomed!"

# The Ultimate Fan' mary-kat

Don't miss

## The New Adventures of MARY-KATE & ASHLEY

- ❏ The Case Of The Great Elephant Escape
- ❏ The Case Of The Summer Camp Caper
- ❏ The Case Of The Surfing Secret
- ❏ The Case Of The Green Ghost
- ❏ The Case Of The Big Scare Mountain Mystery
- ❏ The Case Of The Slam Dunk Mystery
- ❏ The Case Of The Rock Star's Secret

- ❏ The Case Of The Cheerleading Camp Mystery
- ❏ The Case Of The Flying Phantom
- ❏ The Case Of The Creepy Castle
- ❏ The Case Of The Golden Slipper
- ❏ The Case Of The Flapper 'Nappe
- ❏ The Case Of The High Seas Secre
- ❏ The Case Of The Logical I Ranch
- ❏ The Case Of The Dog Camp Mystery

## Starring in

- ❏ Switching Goals
- ❏ Our Lips Are Sealed
- ❏ Winning London

# THE NEW ADVENTURES OF MARY-KATE & ASHLEY™
## Be a Character in a Mary-Kate & Ashley Book Sweepstakes

## OFFICIAL RULES:

1. No purchase necessary.

2. To enter complete the official entry form or hand print your name, address, age, and phone number along with the words "THE NEW ADVENTURES OF MARY-KATE & ASHLEY" Be a Character in a Mary-Kate & Ashley Book Sweepstakes" on a 3"x 5" card and mail to THE NEW ADVENTURES OF MARY-KATE & ASHLEY Be a Character in a Mary-Kate & Ashley Book Sweepstakes, c/o HarperEntertainment, Attn: Children's Marketing Department, 10 East 53rd Street, New York, NY 10022, postmarked **no later than January 31, 2002.** Enter as often as you wish, but each entry must be mailed separately. One entry per envelope. Partially completed, illegible or mechanically reproduced entries will not be accepted. Sponsor, as defined below, is not responsible for lost, late, mutilated, illegible, stolen, postage due, incomplete, or misdirected entries. All entries become the property of Dualstar Entertainment Group, Inc., and will not be returned.

3. Sweepstakes open to all legal residents of the United States (excluding Rhode Island), who are between the ages of five and fifteen by January 31, 2002, excluding employees and immediate family members of HarperCollins Publishers Inc. ("HarperCollins"), Parachute Properties and Parachute Press, Inc., and their respective subsidiaries and affiliates, officers, directors, shareholders, employees, agents, attorneys, and other representatives (individually and collectively "Parachute"), Dualstar Entertainment Group, Inc., and its subsidiaries and affiliates, officers, directors, shareholders, employees, agents, attorneys, and other representatives (individually and collectively "Dualstar"), and their respective parent companies, affiliates, subsidiaries, advertising, promotion and fulfillment agencies, and the persons with whom each of the above are domiciled. Offer void where prohibited or restricted by law.

4. Odds of winning depend on the total number of entries received. All prizes will be awarded. Winners will be randomly drawn on or about February 15, 2002, by HarperEntertainment, whose decisions are final. Potential winners will be notified by mail and will be required to sign and return an affidavit of eligibility and release of liability within 14 days of notification. Prizes won by minors will be awarded to parent or legal guardian who must sign and return all required legal documents. By acceptance of their prize, winners consent to the use of their names, photographs, likeness, and personal information by HarperCollins, Parachute, Dualstar, and for publicity purposes without further compensation except where prohibited.

5.a) One (1) Grand Prize Winner will have his or her name included in a Mary-Kate & Ashley book, as a character; and receive an autographed copy of the book in which the Winner's name appears. HarperCollins, Parachute, and Dualstar reserve the right to substitute another prize of equal or greater value in the event that the winner is unable to receive the prize for any reason. Approximate retail value: $4.25

  b) Fifty (50) First Prize Winners win an autographed Mary-Kate & Ashley book. Approximate total retail value $212.50

6. Only one prize will be awarded per individual, family, or household. Prizes are non-transferable and cannot be sold or redeemed for cash. No cash substitute is available. Any federal, state, or local taxes are the responsibility of the winner. Sponsor may substitute prize of equal or greater value, if necessary, due to availability.

7. Additional terms: By participating, entrants agree a) to the official rules and decisions of the judges, which will be final in all respects; and to waive any claim to ambiguity of the official rules and b) to release, discharge, and hold harmless HarperCollins, Parachute, Dualstar, and their affiliates, subsidiaries, and advertising and promotion agencies from and against any and all liability or damages associated with acceptance, use, or misuse of any prize received in this sweepstakes.

8. Any dispute arising from this Sweepstakes will be determined according to the laws of the State of New York, without reference to its conflict of law principles, and the entrants consent to the personal jurisdiction of the State and Federal courts located in New York County and agree that such courts have exclusive jurisdiction over all such disputes.

9. To obtain the name of the winners, please send your request and a self-addressed stamped envelope (excluding residents of Vermont and Washington) to:

   THE NEW ADVENTURES OF MARY-KATE & ASHLEY™ Be a Character in a Mary-Kate & Ashley Book Sweepstakes
   c/o HarperEntertainment
   10 East 53rd Street, New York, NY 10022
   by March 1, 2002. Sweepstakes sponsor: HarperCollins Publishers, Inc.

# Jet to London
## with Mary-Kate and Ashley!